Mr. Harry's Flowers

By

Rita Kim Will

Dedication

I dedicate this to my dad, Harold, who would have loved this book.

And to my two sons--Zachary and Kirk--always!

About the Author

Rita Kim is a retired teacher who remains active in the lives of children. She uses her writing to reach both children and adults. Rita Kim lives in Nebraska and continues to pursue her passion for writing.

Once there lived a nice old man by the name of Mr. Harry. Every morning, after Mr. Harry got ready for work, he would go outside his tiny white house into the backyard and pick two flowers. Both his front and back yards were covered in flowers of all kinds. He had roses, daisies, irises, pansies, daffodils, carnations, marigolds, lilies of the valley, and tulips.

Harry loved flowers because his wife had once loved them. She had passed away years ago, and when she was alive, they both tended to the flowers daily. Now, Mr. Harry tended to the flowers every day by himself.

After picking his flowers in the morning, he would walk to Joe's café, where he would order black coffee and a bagel with cream cheese. Every day, he sat on the same stool at the end of the counter, and the same waitress, Bella, would wait on him.

"Good morning to you," Bella would say. Sometimes Bella was grumpy when he walked in. He could tell by the look on her face and whether her hair was in a bun—that meant she didn't have enough time to fix it. Today, it was in a bun.

"Good morning, Bella. How are you today?" Mr. Harry would say, and he meant every word of it.

She would tell him what had gone on before she got to work at the café that morning. She had five kids, and getting them all ready for school was hectic. Somehow, once she told him, she felt better, and her whole day improved. The grumpiness was gone!

Mr. Harry would give her one of the flowers before he left and say, "Have a good day, Bella." And he meant every word of it.

Bella added the flower to a big vase because every day, she got a flower, and every day, she was grateful for Mr. Harry, who would take her grumpiness away.

JOE'S
CAFÉ
café

Mr. Harry would then walk the six blocks to work. He would go up to the third floor of the brick office building and into his corner office with two big picture windows, where the sun shone brightly in.

People in the office would stop by to say good morning to Mr. Harry. He would always reply, "Good morning to you. How are you today?" And he meant every word of it.

The people in the office were waiting for Mr. Harry because they would tell him their troubles, and their grumpiness would go away too.

Sarah talked about her son, who was failing in school. John talked about his sick mother and how he was the only one of his siblings who would care for her. Mason talked about the crazy drivers he encountered every day on his way to work, even though they lived in a small town.

They would all talk about their problems, anything that was bothering them, and somehow, their grumpiness would disappear.

Every day, Mr. Harry would choose one person in the office to receive the other flower he had brought. Everyone had a vase on their desks, just waiting for a chance to receive one of his beautiful flowers, because it seemed to brighten their days even more.

At the end of the day, Mr. Harry would pack up his things and head home. People would smile and say, "Good night, Mr. Harry. See you tomorrow." And Mr. Harry would reply, "Good night, have a good night." And he meant it.

Mr. Harry would go home and tend to the flowers. They always needed care—weeding, watering, and nurturing. He did it with loving hands and a tender heart, always thinking of his wife.

Mr. Harry would then have soup and bread for dinner, lay out his clothes for the next morning, read the daily paper, watch TV, and go to bed. He always had a vase with one of the flowers on the nightstand by his bed in honor of his wife.

GOOD
Delicious food
HONEY
COFFEE
Organic Food
MILK
Orange juice

The next day at the office, many people were waiting for Mr. Harry. One person had fought with his son and needed to share that. Another lady had gotten into a fender bender and was late for work; she needed to share that, too. Even the boss that day was grumpy and was waiting for Mr. Harry to talk to.

But Mr. Harry didn't show up for work. He didn't call either. No one seemed to know his phone number or even where he lived. People were getting grumpier and grumpier. No one was smiling. No one was in a good mood, and they were angry at each other.

One person finally said angrily, "Where is Mr. Harry, anyway?"

No one knew.

All at once, the elevator opened, and Bella stepped out. She said, "I am the waitress at Joe's Café. Mr. Harry told me he worked here, and he didn't come in for black coffee and a bagel with cream cheese this morning. I am worried about him. Do you know where he lives? I want to go check on him."

The people in the office looked at each other and felt guilty for being angry, for snapping at each other, and for being grumpy when they should have been worrying more about their friend.

JOE'S CAFE

One man said, "Well, he must live where there are flowers everywhere because he brings in one flower every day."

Bella said, "Yes, you are right because he also brings me one every day."

Another person said, "Well, I know Mr. Harry walks to work, so it can't be too far from here."

The boss said, "We are going to close the office and go check on Mr. Harry." Everyone agreed, and they decided to walk around the small town until they found the house with the flowers.

They broke up into groups. There were four groups of people, and each group was going to walk in one of the four directions—north, south, east, and west—until they found where Mr. Harry lived. Until they found where Mr. Harry's flowers were. Until they knew Mr. Harry was all right. They took off. Each group had a person in charge. There was no arguing, and no one was complaining. They knew this was important.

After about twenty minutes, the group that headed west found a house. Bella was in charge of this group. The house had a white picket fence and a porch with a swing on it. It was a small house, and the yard was covered with flowers, both in the front and in the back! The people were so happy, but they were still worried. They needed to check on Mr. Harry.

Bella ran up to the door, knocked loudly, and yelled, "Mr. Harry, Mr. Harry, are you in there?"

There was no answer.

"Mr. Harry!" she shouted louder and knocked even harder.

There was still no answer. People were looking in the windows, trying to see what was going on. Just as they had decided to break down the door, a neighbor lady came out of her house.

She yelled, "If you are looking for Mr. Harry, he isn't here. He had a heart attack last night, and his daughter took him to the hospital. She called me and said he is doing fine this morning."

None of the people even knew Mr. Harry had a daughter. They were too busy telling him about their own lives to ask him about his. Mr. Harry was such a good listener and a wonderful friend to them, but they were not feeling very good about themselves right now.

"Thank you," Bella said to the neighbor.

They met back up with the other groups at the office. Everyone knew that Mr. Harry probably couldn't have more than one visitor at a time at the hospital, so Bella came up with a plan. She shared her idea with everyone. They were so excited they couldn't wait until the end of the day. Each person had a job to do, and they went about it with love for Mr. Harry.

After working hours, they all met at the hospital. They elected Bella to go up to Mr. Harry's room for them. While she was going into the hospital, they all formed a line outside on the sidewalk.

COUNTY HOSPITAL

"Mr. Harry," Bella said when she walked into his room. She was excited to see that he was sitting up and smiling.

"Bella, my dear, I am so sorry I missed breakfast today!"

"I think I can excuse you this time!" Bella laughed. "Mr. Harry," she said again, "I was wondering if you could look outside your window?"

Mr. Harry's daughter, Lily, walked in just then, and she and Bella helped get Mr. Harry up to look outside the second-story window.

As Mr. Harry looked out, he saw the people all lined up and down the sidewalk. They saw Mr. Harry and started to cheer! What he saw were balloons—lots and lots of balloons—in all of the same colors as his flowers. He saw signs that said, "Get well, Mr. Harry!" and "We love you, Mr. Harry!"

They were waving and smiling, and Mr. Harry waved and smiled back!

Lily said to Bella, "He didn't think anyone would miss him."

The people outside shouted, counted to three, and let the balloons float up to the sky. Mr. Harry was smiling and could hear them yell, "Hurry up and get better, Mr. Harry! We miss you!"

There was a tear in Mr. Harry's eyes as he smiled, waved back, and gave them the thumbs-up sign. He was grateful for his friends, and when they said they missed him, he knew they meant it.

COUNTY HOSPITAL
COUNTY HOSPITAL

The End